MAKE IT
OUT ALIVE
ON A
MOUNTAIN

Claudia Martin

PowerKiDS
press.
New York

Published in 2018 by The Rosen Publishing Group
29 East 21st Street, New York, NY 10010

Produced for Rosen by Calcium
Editors: Sarah Eason and Jennifer Sanderson
Designer: Emma DeBanks
Picture Research: Rachel Blount
Illustrator: Venetia Dean

Picture credits: Cover: Shutterstock: Scott E Read (br), Robsama (bg). Inside: Shutterstock: Africa Studio
20, 47, Galyna Andrushko 13, Dennis W Donohue 28, Dotshock 14, Dutourdumonde Photography 7,
Everst 5, Zadiraka Evgenii 5tr, Franz12 18, John Goldstein 25, Elliot Houghton 15, Images72 21, Jojoo64 22,
Kjetil Kolbjornsrud 26, Vasiliy Koval 12, Andrei Kuzmik 5c, Vaclav Mach 40, Mikadun 36–37, 37b, Monkey
Business Images 41, My Good Images 44, MyImages – Micha 29, NaMaKuKi 5cr, Colombo Nicola 42, Iv
Nikolny 9, OlegDoroshin 16, Tyler Olson 11, Pincasso 19, Daniel Prudek 38, Scott E Read 30, Lysogor Roman
34, Scandphoto 27, Sebartz 24, Taiga 33, VanHart 6, Yojik 32, Yykkaa 10, Zerbor 39r; Wikimedia Commons:
James Heilman, MD 35, LadyofHats 39tl.

Cataloging-in-Publication Data
Names: Martin, Claudia.
Title: Make it out alive on a mountain / Claudia Martin.
Description: New York : PowerKids Press, 2018. | Series: Makerspace survival | Includes index.
Identifiers: ISBN 9781499434781 (pbk.) | ISBN 9781499434729 (library bound) | ISBN 9781499434606 (6
pack)
Subjects: LCSH: Wilderness survival--Juvenile literature. | Mountaineering--Juvenile literature.
Classification: LCC GV200.52 M35 2018 | DDC 796.522--dc23

Manufactured in China.

CPSIA Compliance Information: Batch BS17PK: For Further Information contact Rosen Publishing, New
York, New York at 1-800-237-9932

Please note that the publisher **does not**
suggest readers carry out any practical
application of the Can You Make It?
activities and any other survival
activities in this book.

A note about measurements:
Measurements are given in U.S. form with
metric in parentheses. The metric conversion
is rounded to make it easier to measure.

CONTENTS

CHAPTER 1

SURVIVE
THE MOUNTAINS

You are about to be parachuted onto a ridge in one of the world's highest and most remote mountain ranges. From there, you must make your own way back to civilization. As if that were not difficult enough, here are the rules: You cannot take any food, drinks, a tent, fire starters, or cooking equipment with you. How will you survive?

Will You Make It Out Alive?

You can set out with just a few belongings. You can dress in your choice of clothes and footwear. You can also carry a pocketknife. Apart from these essentials, you will have to provide yourself with food, water, and shelter by making your own tools and equipment. You are allowed to use any local materials you can find in the mountains, as well as any recyclable man-made items you can spot. You will also be provided with a backpack in which you will find some interesting materials and tools.

> You are about to embark on a mountain adventure. Are you ready for it?

What Is in Your Backpack?

The following materials and tools are in your backpack. When you come across a "Can You Make It?" activity in this book, you must choose from this list of items to construct it. Each item can be used only once. Study the list carefully before you set off. You can find the correct solutions for all the activities on page 45 of this book.

Can You Make It?

Materials
- 2 ropes, 18 feet (5 m) long each
- 12 garden stakes
- 24 plastic twist ties
- Canvas tarp, 10 x 12 feet (3 x 4 m), with eyelets at each corner
- Duct tape
- Large, thick cardboard box
- Plastic garbage bag
- Plastic sealable odor-free bag
- Poultry netting
- Sack
- Small-holed netting

Tools
- Craft knife
- Pair of scissors
- Wire cutters

Rope

Plastic ties

Wire cutters

Survival Tip
Use the Internet to look up all the items in your backpack before you begin your journey. Make sure you understand what they are and how you might be able to use them.

5

WORLD OF MOUNTAINS

Before setting off, it is important that you understand the dangers of the **terrain** you will be facing. Cliffs, ice-covered slopes, and river-filled ravines will block your route. At high **altitude**, it will be icy cold, and you will come across only the hardiest humans, animals, and plants.

Great Ranges

Earth's outer layer, or crust, is formed by **tectonic plates**. These plates created the world's mountain ranges by forcing up the land like crumpled paper. The world's highest range is the Himalayas in Asia. There, you will find the world's tallest peak, Mount Everest, at 29,029 feet (8,848 m). The longest mountain range, not including those beneath the seas, is the Andes, which stretches for about 4,300 miles (7,000 km) down South America.

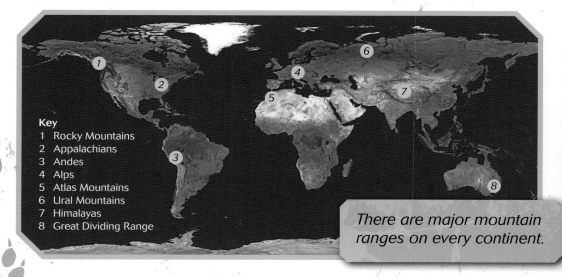

Key
1 Rocky Mountains
2 Appalachians
3 Andes
4 Alps
5 Atlas Mountains
6 Ural Mountains
7 Himalayas
8 Great Dividing Range

There are major mountain ranges on every continent.

Mountain Landscape

The higher up a mountain you hike, the more **inhospitable** the weather and landscape become. On the lower slopes, the plants and animals are similar to those that live in surrounding valleys. Higher up, as the air cools, the **dominant** plants are coniferous trees, such as firs, which bear cones and needle-shaped leaves. These are the only trees that can survive the cold and short growing season.

As you journey higher, the forest peters out as you cross the **timberline**. The timberline is the name for the altitude above which trees cannot survive, and it varies from region to region. Above this point, you will find no wood for your campfire or shelter. The terrain is rocky and windswept. Yet higher is the **snow line**. Above this, the ground is covered in snow all year. Only the hardiest animals, such as snow leopards, yaks, and snow partridges, spend a long time above the snow line. Only plants like **cold-adapted** mosses hide beneath the ice.

The timberline and snow line can be seen on the slopes of Annapurna I, which is in the Himalayas.

MOUNTAIN
PEOPLES

Mountains are hostile environments in which to make a home, but some peoples do exactly that. The Sherpa people live on the slopes of the Himalayas at altitudes of up to 14,000 feet (4,300 m). Before you leave for the mountains, pick up some tips from the maker skills of the Sherpa.

Sturdy Builds

Traditional Sherpa herd animals such as yaks, which have long, thick woolen coats. They also plant crops such as maize and vegetables on flat terraces cut from the mountainside. At this altitude, where snow covers the ground from November to February, a main concern is how to build **sturdy**, warm houses.

Sherpa homes are often built into the mountainside. The mountainside provides warmth and shelter from fierce winds. Roofs are sloping, so that snow and rain slide off, rather than collapse the structure with their weight. All the windows face in the direction of the sun to warm the inside. At the center of the house is the fireplace. The outer house wall is constructed from stone. Inside this strong barrier is a narrow, air-filled gap for **insulation**, then an inner wooden frame. Air is a good insulator if it can be trapped, since it is slow to transfer heat.

FIERCE FACT!
The Sherpa are renowned mountaineering guides. The first climbers to reach the summit of Mount Everest were Sherpa Tenzing Norgay and New Zealander Edmund Hillary, in 1953.

8

Fabulous Fibers

Traditional Sherpa clothing is made from thickly woven yak wool or sheepskin. The same properties that allow these animals to survive in the mountains are ideal for keeping the Sherpa warm and dry. Yak wool and sheepskin are excellent insulators, as they trap air among their **fibers**. The fibers can also **absorb** a large quantity of water, then release it into the air, keeping the wearer dry. This property is called wicking moisture.

Sherpa wear several layers of clothes, as well as woolen hats, to trap heat.

9

MOUNTAIN
SURVIVOR

In 2013, 23-year-old hiker Mary Owen set off to climb 11,249-foot (3,429 m) Mount Hood, in Oregon. She was lightly dressed and had few supplies. What started as a fair-weather day trip turned into a six-day battle against the elements. Mary's maker skills kept her alive.

Disaster Strikes

Mary was 1,000 feet (305 m) from the summit when a **blizzard** hit. Within minutes, she was in a **whiteout**, unable to see farther than a foot ahead. Turning downhill, she lost her way and entered a steep, rocky canyon. Then Mary fell, tumbling 40 feet (12 m) and gashing her leg, leaving her unable to walk.

Immediately, Mary dug herself a snow cave. A snow cave is a hollow in the snow. It provides insulation and shelter from the chill of the wind. She expected rescuers to find her soon because she had filled in a form at the ranger's office when she set off, detailing her route. Mary did not know that her form had been lost.

Dig a hole in the snow for warmth.

Making Use of Supplies

As the days passed, Mary used the materials she had. She stretched out her small supply of food: Energy bars, crackers, and noodles. She lit a fire with twigs and the **flammable** wrappers from her energy bars. She used this to warm her hands and dry her clothes. For drinking water, Mary gathered snow in her water bottle and left it in the sun to melt. When it rained, she collected water in her waterproof plastic poncho. During daylight hours, Mary dragged herself onto a ridge, so that rescue helicopters could spot her. It was not until the sixth day that one finally did. Mary's college roommate had called the police when she realized Mary was missing, four days after her fall.

Being able to start a fire, even with wet materials, is a very important survival skill. Make sure you master it.

CHAPTER 2
KEEP WARM

You have been dropped on a mountain peak, far from any **settlement** or road. It is bitterly cold, and when you take into account the **wind chill factor** and the increased risk of rain and snow, it is clear that keeping yourself warm is your first priority.

Why So Cold and Wet?
As altitude increases, the air becomes thinner. This makes it harder to breathe at high altitudes. When air is thinner, it is less able to absorb and hold onto heat. On average, the temperature drops by up to 5° F (3° C) for every 1,000 feet (305 m) you climb.

Mountains are usually rainier than their surrounding regions. Winds carry moist air over the land. When the air reaches a mountain, it rises and cools. Cool air is able to hold less moisture than warm air, so it may fall as rain or snow.

Fingerless gloves are warm and also allow the climber to feel for handholds.

Designing Clothing

Until well into the twentieth century, climbers and hikers followed the example of mountain peoples, such as the Sherpa, when choosing clothing. They used animal fibers such as wool, feathers, and furs. The problem was that it was necessary to wear many layers of these thick fabrics, making it difficult to move. No animal fiber performs well when soaked through.

From the mid-twentieth century, makers studied the properties of animal fibers to develop man-made fibers that are insulating, waterproof, lightweight, and flexible. One of these fibers was Gore-Tex, which was developed by Wilbert and Robert Gore in 1969. Gore-Tex is a man-made polymer. Polymers are substances that look like chains when seen under a microscope. Gore-Tex fibers are full of minute holes. They are too small for raindrops to pass through but big enough to allow the wearer's skin to breathe, so that it does not feel sweaty. Gore-Tex is used for the outer layer of mountain clothing.

FIERCE FACT!
One of the fastest winds ever recorded was measured at the summit of Mount Washington, in New Hampshire. It was 231 miles per hour (372 km/h).

Have you chosen the right clothes for your mountain challenge? What materials are they made from?

FIRE STARTER

Build a fire to warm up and dry your clothes, as well as to cook food and boil water. Lighting a fire in wet and windy conditions requires an understanding of your available materials as well as construction skills.

Make a Tinder Nest

Tinder is any dry material that will burn easily. Good tinder includes dried grass, wood shavings, pine needles, bark, or moss. If your tinder is wet, rub it quickly between your hands. The **friction** will slowly dry it out. Form your dry tinder into a small bundle, or nest.

Create a Spark

Since you do not have matches or a lighter, you must use another method to create a spark. In strong sunshine, use a magnifying glass, glasses lens, or binocular lens to concentrate the sun's rays on your tinder nest. Hold the lens in place until the heat makes the tinder smoke and flame.

If it is cloudy, you will need to hunt for flints. Flints and similar spark-producing rocks have a smooth appearance and may be split like broken glass. They can often be found along riverbeds. Scrape your flint with your pocketknife or other steel object to make sparks. Direct the sparks onto your tinder nest, blowing gently to feed the flame.

Feed your fire gently. Throwing on too much fuel at once could smother it.

Construct a Tepee Fire

A tried and true fire-construction method is the tepee. Over your flaming tinder nest, form a tepee shape out of small sticks. Fire needs oxygen to burn, so give your flames room to breathe. Then, construct a second tepee out of larger, longer sticks over the first, leaving space between the two layers. To prevent your fire from burning out of control in dry conditions, dig a campfire pit, surround it with rocks, and then clear the nearby area of vegetation.

Learn to construct a tepee fire. Once it is blazing, warm your hands and dry your clothes.

BUILD
A SHELTER

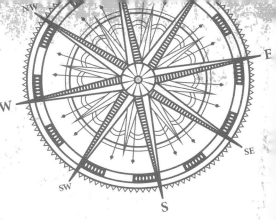

If night is falling or your clothes are wet, make a shelter quickly. Your design will depend on your environment and available materials. Consider whether you can make use of natural features, such as sheltering rocks or a thick group of trees, as a framework.

A Lean-To

A lean-to shelter is one of the simplest and quickest shelters to construct with limited materials. A lean-to is supported on one side by trees, posts, or other props. On the other side, its roof slopes down to the ground. This type of shelter has the drawback of offering protection from wind and rain in only one direction. However, if you build your lean-to facing your campfire, it will be surprisingly warm.

If you are armed with an ax or other cutting tool, a lean-to shelter can be constructed using only branches, leaves, and other found materials.

Make a Lean-To

From your list of supplies and some local materials, you will need to make:

➜ A lean-to shelter that protects you from the wind but faces the warmth from your campfire

➜ A waterproof roof for your shelter and a means of attaching your shelter to trees or other posts.

Can You Make It?

Step 1
Consider which item you will use to create the roof of your lean-to.

Step 2
You will need to find two suitably positioned trees or two sturdy branches that can be driven into the ground. Which item will you use to secure your shelter to your posts?

Step 3
How high off the ground do you think the open side of your lean-to should be? Think about factors such as wind, warmth, and sleeping space.

Step 4
Which local materials could be used to weigh down the side of your lean-to that touches the ground?

Roof

Posts

Local materials to weigh down the lean-to

CHAPTER 3
FIND FOOD

Now that you have constructed your fire and shelter, think about meeting your other vital survival needs: Drinking water and eating food. Put your maker skills into action to construct your essential kit, using only found and recycled materials.

Boiling Point

In the mountains, your best sources of drinking water are streams, snow, and ice. Look for streams that have traveled through areas without human habitation, which could have polluted the water. Make sure snow and ice look pearly white. You still need to purify your water before drinking. The simplest method is to bring water to the boiling point over your campfire. Keep it boiling for at least 60 seconds. If you are at an altitude of more than 6,500 feet (1,980 m), increase the boiling time to 3 minutes, since water boils at a lower temperature the higher your go.

The best container for boiling water is metal, perhaps a pot, cup, or empty food can. If you cannot find these items, water can be boiled in a plastic, bark, or paper container. Make sure you keep your container full of water, and watch it closely for signs of melting, smoking, or burning.

To hang a cooking pot, drive two forked branches into the ground. Balance a crossbeam between them.

Stick Out!

If you cannot find a cooking pot, you must master another method of cooking food. A simple option is to skewer meat, fish, or vegetables on a stick, then hold the food over the fire. To give your arms a rest, push two Y-shaped sticks into the ground beside your fire. Balance your skewers on them. You will have to experiment with different heights and positions.

Rest your skewers over a Y-shaped wooden frame.

FIERCE FACT!

Boiling water kills any **parasites** and **bacteria**. The parasite *Giardia*, found in animal droppings, is common in streams and lakes in the United States.

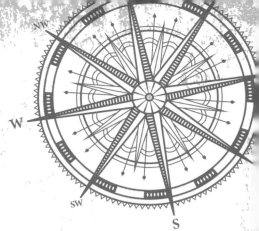

ROOTING
FOR ROOTS

There are more than 20,000 types of **edible** plants in the world, and many are found in the mountains. If you know where to look, you can harvest roots, nuts, seeds, and berries. However, many mountain plants and **fungi** are poisonous, so **forage** only with the help of a knowledgeable adult.

A Basketful

Although mushrooms and toadstools are abundant in mountain forests, the safest choice is to leave them completely alone. Several **species** are poisonous and are nearly impossible to tell apart from their harmless cousins. Also avoid any plants or berries that you do not recognize, particularly anything growing on a plant with red or white leaves, hairs, or spines. In summer and early fall, if an adult can identify blackberries or raspberries, they are packed with vitamins. Construct a basket for your harvest by weaving reeds or flexible branches in a simple over and under pattern.

In the summer, you can forage for blackberries on the lower slopes of most mountain ranges.

Roots and Tubers

Some plants store food in swollen roots and **tubers** beneath the soil. One plant with edible roots is common chicory, which has bright blue flowers. The roots can be harvested from fall to spring, but an adult must check them, and they must be boiled before eating.

Spades

To construct a survival spade for digging up roots, choose a sturdy **hardwood** stick. North American hardwood species include maple, hickory, oak, or walnut. Sharpen your stick with your pocketknife, directing your cuts away from your body and hands. Use the sharpened stick to strike into the soil to loosen it, then scrape away the debris with a flat rock.

FIERCE FACT!
The oldest baskets are around 12,000 years old. People were probably weaving baskets thousands of years earlier, but their **organic** materials decayed long ago.

Common chicory is easiest to identify from late spring to fall, while its flowers are in bloom.

LEAPING FISH

Mountain streams are teaming with fish such as bass, salmon, and trout. For thousands of years, people have been constructing traps to catch river fish. Catch and keep only what you need, and return the rest of your fish to the river.

River Fish Trap

The key to constructing a fish trap is that the open side of the trap should face **upstream**, so that fish will swim inside. Once inside, the flow of the water will prevent fish from escaping.

The simplest traps can be formed by a series of tall, closely spaced sticks driven upright into the stream bed, forming a cone-shaped enclosure, or funnel, from which fish cannot escape. A cone-shaped basket of woven branches also creates an effective trap. When making a trap, bear in mind that although fish should not be able to swim out of it, water should be able to flow through it, so that the trap is not destroyed or washed away by the force of the current.

*Traditional fish traps are constructed from organic materials that are strong but **pliable**.*

Make It Out Alive

Make a Fish Trap

From your list of supplies, you will need to make:

→ A fish trap with a rigid, box-shaped frame
→ A funnel through which fish enter the trap when swimming downstream
→ A holding area for fish that swim through the funnel, from which they cannot escape.

Can You Make It?

Step 1

Consider which items you will use to create the box-shaped frame for your trap. Which items could be used to tie together your frame?

Step 2

Which item could form a strong entrance funnel? The large end of your funnel needs to be attached to your frame. The smaller end needs to be wide enough for fish to swim into the holding area.

Step 3

Which item could cover the frame to prevent fish from escaping from the holding area? Attach this material around the edge of your funnel, and cover the other five sides of the frame.

Step 4

Before completely securing your frame's cover, which local materials could be placed inside your trap to weigh it down?

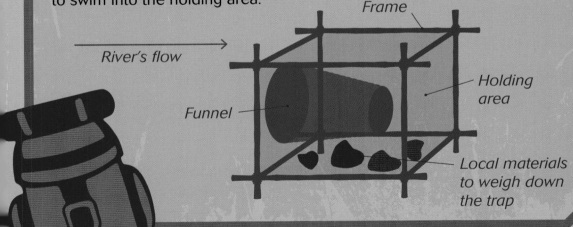

River's flow

Frame

Funnel

Holding area

Local materials to weigh down the trap

CHAPTER 4

BEAST ATTACK

Alone in the mountains, you are at risk from some of nature's deadliest predators, which are adapted to hunting down prey in this challenging terrain. Since humankind's earliest days, we have put our maker skills to the test to protect ourselves from wild beasts.

Mountain Predators

Predators that live in the mountains have developed characteristics that help them cope with the rugged landscape and at the highest altitudes, cold temperatures, and thinner air. The mountain predators that are large enough to be a danger to humans include members of the bear family; the cat family, such as cougars and snow leopards; and the Canidae family, which includes wolves and coyotes. These animals have strong jaws and sharp teeth; a powerful sense of smell; strong muscles for leaping and climbing; and thick fur. Some are lone hunters, such as the cougar, while others roam their territory in packs.

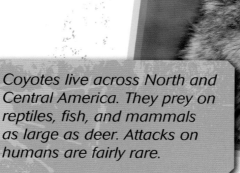

Coyotes live across North and Central America. They prey on reptiles, fish, and mammals as large as deer. Attacks on humans are fairly rare.

24

Build to Survive

As early as 500,000 years ago, long before modern humans had evolved, our ancestors had figured out how to construct spears with sharp stone tips and wooden shafts. These were for hunting and protection. The dark nights were when our ancestors were most at risk from beast attacks. Before they learned to construct permanent shelters, many of our ancestors retreated into caves to sleep, protecting the entrance with a fence of sharp sticks and smoking fires. Some groups climbed trees, where they made simple nests among the branches. During your mountain challenge, take some tips from the skills of your ancestors.

A tree house made from wood, rope, and nails makes use of the natural protection offered by a sturdy tree.

WOLF PACK

The gray wolf is the largest member of the Canidae family, reaching 63 inches (160 cm) long and 34 inches (86 cm) across the shoulders. This wolf lives in packs in the wilderness areas of North America, Europe, and Asia. It is just possible you may meet gray wolves in the mountains.

Wolves live in packs made up of one or more families. Packs as large as 40 are known.

Skilled Hunter

Thousands of years of interaction with humans has taught gray wolves that people can be dangerous, so wolf attacks are rare. However, in remote areas where wolves are unused to humans, or during times when food is scarce, children and smaller adults should know how to defend themselves.

Wolves track prey by its scent, stalking then chasing the prey down in a final rush. If prey is in a group, wolves will single out smaller and slower individuals. Animals as large as bison and musk oxen are killed.

Your Best Defense

If you are attacked, do not run. Back away slowly while keeping eye contact with the animal. Make yourself seem powerful by raising your arms and making loud noises. If you are cornered, back up against a tree, grab a stick, and fight back.

At night, turn to your maker skills for defense. Wolves are afraid of flames and smoke. Light a circle of fires around your camp, using green leaves and damp wood to make smoke. Construct a defensive fence. Wolves can jump at least 8 feet (2 m) high, so you are unlikely to build tall enough to keep them out. Instead, think about making it difficult for wolves to get across your barrier. Use sharpened sticks with their points inclined outward, as well as rocks and tangled foliage-covered branches.

Tie sharpened sticks into your defensive fence, using strips of bark or branches as rope.

FIERCE FACT!
By the 1930s, wolves had almost disappeared from the lower 48 US states. They have been reintroduced to several states, giving a population of about 5,600, plus 7,700 in Alaska.

27

COUGAR AMBUSH

The cougar, also called a mountain lion or puma, hunts at night, so avoid walking in cougar territory after the sun has dipped. This big cat is found from northern Canada, down through the Rockies, to the southern Andes in South America.

Cougars have large paws and strong legs, making them agile jumpers and climbers.

Know Your Enemy

A cougar is most likely to harm you if it feels cornered. If you do come across one, do not run, do not scream, do not stand still, and do not pretend to be dead. All these reactions will make the cougar think you are easy prey. Instead, back away slowly while shouting in a deep, firm voice. Jump on top of a rock to appear tall, and without bending down, grab a branch to shake and defend yourself with.

Construct an Air Horn

If you have an air horn ready in your pocket, blasting it may startle a cougar into running away. Air horns work by **compressing** air, forcing it through a small hole, which makes a loud noise. If you can find the materials, make a horn using a plastic medicine jar or film canister, a balloon, a drinking straw, and two rubber bands.

Cut a hole in the lid of the medicine jar and another hole in the side of the jar. In the base of the jar, make a hole exactly the width of the drinking straw. Take off the lid of the jar, and stretch a piece of cut balloon tightly over the opening, securing it with a rubber band. Put the lid back on. Stretch and secure a piece of balloon over the base of the jar. Press the drinking straw through this balloon and into the hole. Now blow through the hole in the side of the jar.

This air horn works by pulling out then pressing a plunger. This compresses air in the tube, sending it through the horn with a blast.

FIERCE FACT!
Since 1890, there have been around 90 cougar attacks on people in North America. Attacks are most likely where human settlement threatens cougar territory.

BEAR NECESSITIES

Three bear species are found in North America: black bears, brown bears, and polar bears, which live only in the Arctic. Encounters between humans and black or brown bears do take place in mountain regions and national parks, so be prepared.

Powerful Predator

Brown and black bears are powerful predators, feeding on animals such as fish, deer, and moose. However, much of their diet is made up of nuts, berries, fruit, seeds, and roots. Despite their huge size, bears can run at 30 miles per hour (48 km/h). They may be dangerous to humans if they are surprised or, in the case of female bears, if they are caring for cubs.

North American brown bears are often called grizzlies because their brown fur can be white-tipped, or grizzled. They live in Canada and the northwestern United States.

Protect Your Food

When you set up camp in the mountains, bears can be a serious threat. They smell food from a great distance and will enter your camp to look for it. To keep bears at bay, store your food in a sealed bag high above the ground.

Make a Food Bag

From your list of supplies, you will need to make:

→ One sealable food bag that can store your food hygienically
→ One sling with a weight that is heavy enough to match your stored food once in the bag.

Can You Make It?

Step 1
Consider which item you will need to use to create your food bag.

Step 2
What item will you use to make the sling? What item will you use to attach the sling and food bag to, to hang them from a tree?

Step 3
What local materials could you use for your sling weight?

Step 4
Once your food bag and sling are complete, you will need to find a tree from which to hang them. They will need to be at least 10 feet (3 m) from the nearest tree trunk and at least 12 feet (4 m) above the ground.

Sling

Food bag

10 ft. (3 m)

12 ft. (4 m)

FIERCE FACT!

Bears have been known to leap from tree trunks to snatch food bags. Black bears can reach nearly 10 feet (3 m) high without jumping!

CHAPTER 5
KNOW THE DANGER

In the mountains, the terrain itself poses one of the greatest risks to your safety. Cliffs, canyons, and crevasses are some of the physical hazards along your route. Avalanches, rockfalls, and storms can strike with little warning.

Stormy Weather

Thunderstorms are common in the mountains because mountains force warm air to rise. As it rises, the air cools, and the moisture it holds **condenses** into clouds. Thunderclouds form when clouds grow tall and their water droplets freeze into ice crystals. The crystals brush against each other, creating **static electricity**. The electricity builds up into sparks of lightning.

Watch out for landslides after heavy rain, which may have loosened the soil.

A lightning strike can be deadly. If you hear thunder on an exposed mountainside, you are at risk of a strike. Move away from electrical or metal objects. Stay away from ridges, water, and tall trees. All these things can attract lightning. If your hair stands on end, you are about to be struck. Minimize your contact with the ground, as the electricity will travel across the earth. Instead, squat on the balls of your feet, and put your head between your knees.

When you see an approaching storm, climb down from exposed rocky peaks.

Franklin's Lightning Rod

The heat generated by lightning can set fire to structures made of most materials. In 1749, Benjamin Franklin became the first maker to construct a lightning rod. The principle of a lightning rod, or **conductor**, is to attract the lightning and carry it harmlessly into the ground rather than through a building. Lightning tends to strike the highest object, so lightning rods stand taller than surrounding structures. Rods are made of materials that conduct, or carry, electricity well. Metals such as copper and aluminum are ideal for the task.

FIERCE FACT!

A lightning strike contains 300 million **volts** of electricity, which is enough power to illuminate a light bulb for a whole year.

AVALANCHE ALERT

An avalanche is when a slab of snow slips down a mountainside at high speed, burying everything in its path. These deadly events are caused by sun warming the snow, sudden heavy snowfalls, or just the weight of a walker's feet.

Deadly Danger

If you spot an avalanche heading your way, take cover behind a large rock or outcrop. If you are swept away, try to reach the edge of the flow using swimming motions. If the worst should happen and the avalanche buries you, quickly clear a breathing space in front of your face before the snow sets. If you are near the surface, you may be able to dig your own way out. If not, you will have to wait to be rescued.

Every year, more than 150 people die in avalanches around the world. Skiers and climbers are most at risk.

A Maker Solution

In the 1970s, a German hunter named Josef Hohenester was carrying a dead **chamois** on his back when an avalanche swept him away. Hohenester expected to be buried alive, but the chamois kept him on the surface of the snow. To understand the principle, put sand, gravel, and stones in a bucket. Shake the bucket around. Although you might expect otherwise, you will notice that the larger objects, the stones, rise to the surface of the contents.

The chamois had turned Hohenester into a larger object, keeping him on the surface. Over the years, Hohenester developed on this insight, experimenting with air canisters and, eventually, air bags. Today, many skiers and snowboarders wear air bags, which they inflate in the event of an avalanche.

This skier is demonstrating his air bags. They are a more practical solution than a chamois!

FIERCE FACT!

In the past 25 years, more than 260 people have inflated an air bag during an avalanche. Around 97 percent of them survived.

CRAZY CREVASSES

Glaciers are large masses of ice that form where snowfall is packed layer upon layer, high in mountain ranges. Glaciers move slowly downhill, causing deep cracks in the ice called crevasses. These are perhaps the greatest mountain danger you will face.

Do Not Fall In

The largest crevasses may be 150 feet (46 m) deep, yet they are often extremely thin. Mountain climbers who fall into a crevasse may die from the fall itself. Others may die from hypothermia, or extreme loss of body heat, as they wait for rescue.

Climbers crossing a glacier link themselves together with a rope. They are also armed with ice axes, which can be driven into ice as an anchor. There should be at least 50 feet (15 m) of rope between each climber. This means that if one climber falls, the next climber has time to strike in his ice ax, so he is not dragged into the crevasse by the weight of his companion.

Crevasse Rescue

Over the decades, climbers have used their knowledge of forces and pulleys to perfect the equipment for crevasse rescue. First of all, the weight of the fallen climber needs to be transferred away from the next climber on the line. This is done by hammering two anchors, called pickets, into the ice, then attaching ropes from these to the victim's rope. The free climber detaches himself from his fallen companion.

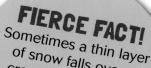

The free climber then attaches a series of pulleys to the rope holding the victim. Pulleys are wheels with grooves around the edge to guide a rope. They are simple machines for lifting weights. Using two pulleys halves the force needed to lift a weight, because two sections of rope, rather than one, support the weight.

Some of these climbers are using sharp-pointed poles, which help them to balance on the ice.

Sometimes, mountain rescue helicopters perform crevasse rescues. The victim is winched to safety.

A KNOTTY PROBLEM

If you are making your way across a crevasse-pocked glacier or climbing a crag, an understanding of ropes and knots is essential. Knots are a useful skill for any maker, whether you are tying together a shelter or a rope ladder.

Rope Climber

The Prusik, named after its inventor, Austrian mountaineer Karl Prusik, is an essential mountaineering knot to master. It is used to attach a loop of cord to a piece of rope. Once attached, the loop can slide up the rope but will not slip when the loop is pulled downward, tightening the knot. In this way, Prusik loops are used to climb up a rope.

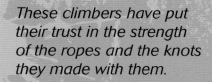

These climbers have put their trust in the strength of the ropes and the knots they made with them.

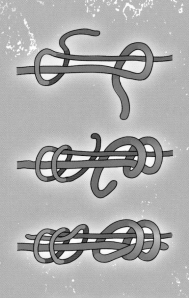

Tying the Knot

To tie the Prusik, make a loop by joining the ends of a cord securely. This is done with a double fisherman's knot. Lay the two ends one above the other, overlapping by a few inches. Wrap one end around both cords, making two full turns, then pass this end back through the turns, pulling tight. Do the same with the other end: Wrap it twice around both cords, and pull tight. Pull on both ends to tighten the two knots.

The Prusik

Now you must attach the loop to the rope. Lay your loop under the rope and at right angles to it. Wrap one side of the loop around the rope and through itself three or four times. Pull the loop out to the side to tighten the wraps. Make sure the wraps are not crossed, or they will not grip the rope tightly.

FIERCE FACT!

The famous Carrick-a-Rede rope bridge in Northern Ireland spans 66 feet (20 m) between the mainland and an island. Many tourists are too afraid to cross it!

You can experiment with the Prusik using just a rubber band and a pencil. Think about what uses you could find for a Prusik knot.

CHAPTER 6
GET MOVING

If you are traveling above the snow line, you could sink waist deep in a snowdrift or slip on hard, brittle ice. Think about how to equip yourself to survive this environment. Will you tramp in snowshoes or sweep over the slopes on skis?

Skiing Through Time

Although skiing did not become popular as a sport until the nineteenth century, people have been gliding over snow on runners attached to their feet for thousands of years. The oldest skis discovered by archaeologists were found in Russia, are made of wood, and date back to 5000 BC. The skis were bound to the wearer's feet by leather or cloth. In the past, the two skis in a pair were not always of equal size. One ski was a long, flat runner, treated with animal fat to reduce friction, which is the force that slows down the motion of a material as it moves against another. The other ski was shorter and used for kicking the skier along.

These old skis are made of wood, leather, and iron. What materials are skis made from today?

Sporty Design

After skiing became a well-loved sport, makers turned their attention to designing skis that were stronger, lighter, faster, flexible, and easier to maneuver. A breakthrough came in 1950, when Howard Head developed a ski with a light plywood core, **laminated** in strong but flexible aluminum. The ski had hard steel edges to help with turning and a tough plastic cover that could be waxed. The wax reduces friction over the snow, so the skis can slide more smoothly.

In 1937, while in the hospital after breaking his leg in a skiing accident, Hjalmar Havam decided it was time to come up with a safer ski binding, which would attach boots securely to skis while skiing but would release the boots in a fall. His clips held the boot in place until a twisting force was applied, caused by a fall. Similar clip bindings are still used today.

A ski is not quite rectangular, and its tip and tail curl upward. Why do you think this is?

GO DOWNHILL

Sleds are vehicles that carry passengers over ice and snow. They may be pulled along by dogs or reindeer, or travel downhill under only the force of **gravity**. Luge is the sport of sledding down high-speed runs on specially designed streamlined sleds.

Toboggan Ride

A toboggan is a simple sled that does not have runners or skis on its underside. Store-bought toboggans are usually made from wood or plastic. They are often in the form of a sideways J shape, with a curled-up front end. You have already examined the shape, materials, and properties that make skis easy to maneuver and reduce friction as they slide over the snow. Bear these factors in mind when you construct your own toboggan to carry you swiftly down a snowy slope.

Dogsled racing is a popular sport in the world's cold regions. Sleds are made from lightweight aluminum.

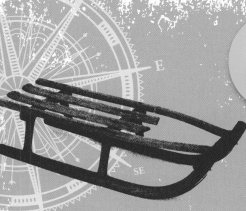

Make a Toboggan

From your list of supplies, you will need to make:

→ *A toboggan that has a streamlined shape*
→ *A fairly comfortable area to sit on*
→ *A smooth cover for your toboggan to reduce friction and make it waterproof.*

Can You Make It?

Step 1
Consider which item you will use to create the basic shape of your toboggan. Will you cut, fold, or stick this item to change its shape?

Step 2
Think about where you will sit. Is the seating area large enough and comfortable enough?

Step 3
Which item will you use to wrap your toboggan to reduce friction over the snow? How will you stick your cover to the base?

Step 4
Test your toboggan. Do you need to make any modifications to increase its speed or comfort?

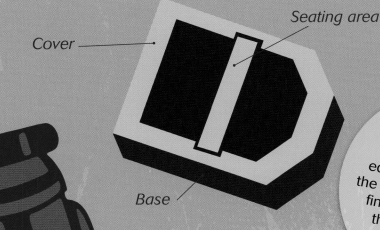

Cover

Seating area

Base

FIERCE FACT!
Lugers wear gloves equipped with spikes on the tips of the middle three fingers. The spikes grip the ice as the lugers launch themselves into a run.

43

WALK AWAY

You will make slow progress above the snow line if you are wearing sneakers. Your toes will also be at risk from **frostbite** as the cold and damp seep through to your skin. To protect your feet, you could make use of a range of found materials to construct snowshoes, including unwanted tennis rackets.

You Made It Out Alive!

Wearing your improvised snowshoes, you tramp downhill past the snow line. Here, the going gets easier, as you remove your snowshoes and make for the shelter of the timberline. Now you follow a mountain stream as it winds its way down the valley, toward the nearest settlement. You have survived your mountain adventure! Along the way, you have armed yourself with the knowledge, skills, and equipment to make another trip to the mountains!

Snowshoes keep you from sinking into the snow by spreading your weight over a larger area. Construct your own using old tennis rackets or bent willow branches tied with duct tape.